KU-186-164

This book belongs to

The Classic Treasury of Best~Loved

Bedtime Stories

Retold by Steven Zorn

Illustrated by Penny Dann

RP|KIDS
CLASSICS
PHILADELPHIA • LONDON

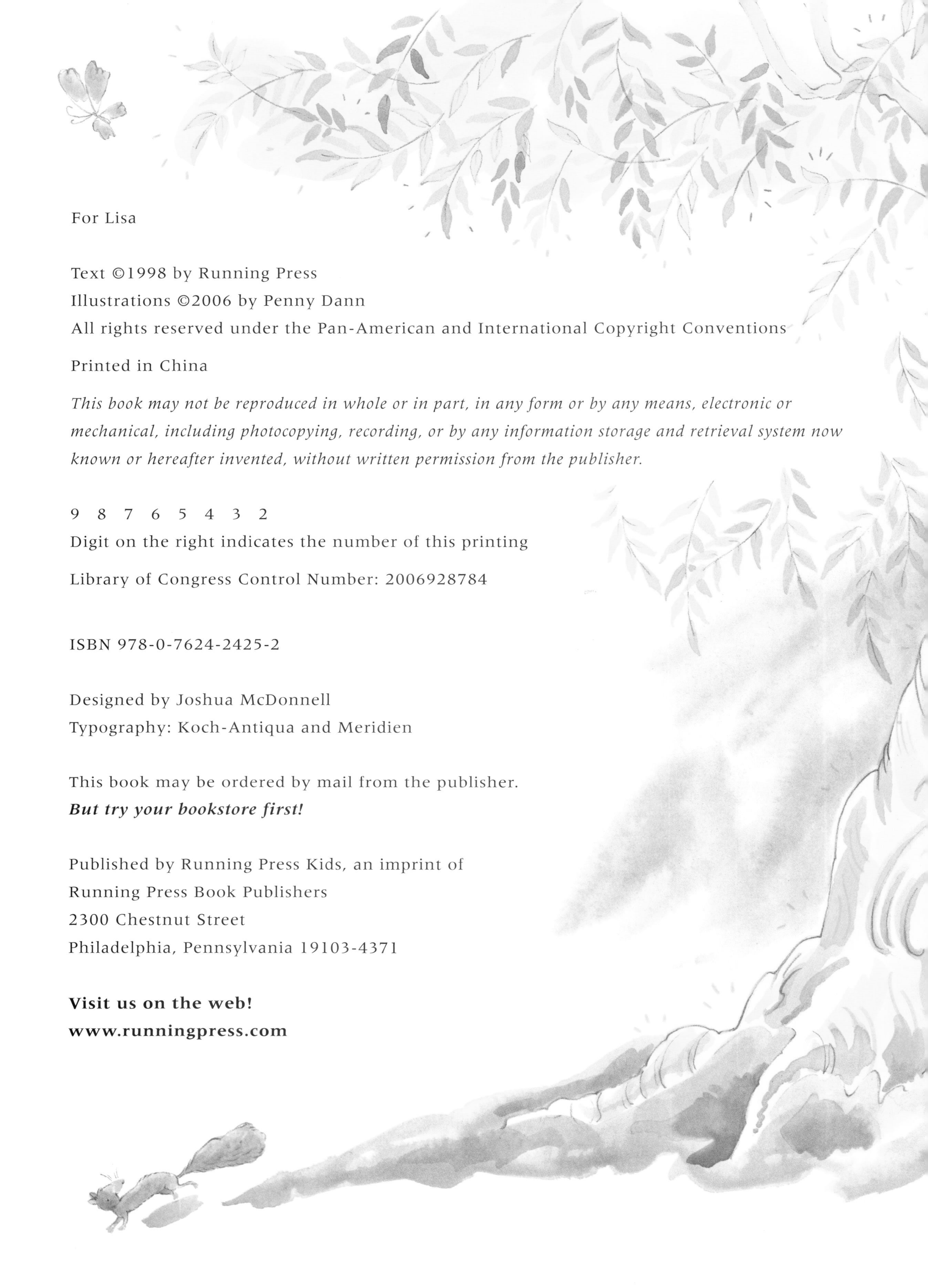

For Lisa

Printed in China

9 8 7 6 5 4 3 2
Digit on the right indicates the number of this printing

Library of Congress Control Number: 2006928784

ISBN 978-0-7624-2425-2

Designed by Joshua McDonnell
Typography: Koch-Antiqua and Meridien

This book may be ordered by mail from the publisher.
But try your bookstore first!

Published by Running Press Kids, an imprint of
Running Press Book Publishers
2300 Chestnut Street
Philadelphia, Pennsylvania 19103-4371

Visit us on the web!
www.runningpress.com

Contents

Introduction

A bedtime story is like a bridge to the land of dreams. It's a way to say goodnight to the everyday world and hello to the amazing universe of the imagination. Like a dream, anything can happen in a bedtime story. You can visit strange lands, meet kings and princesses, go on thrilling adventures—all while you're safely snuggled up in your bed!

Classic bedtime stories never grow old. They're reborn with every child, and each generation finds them as fresh as when they were first told—a long time ago, further back than anyone can remember.

On these pages, you'll find favorite bedtime stories, and maybe some you've never heard before. Here are fantastic tales of talking animals, magical watches, mountains of shimmering glass, and wishes come true. But even with all their enchantment and wizardry, these stories are mostly about honesty, friendship, courage, and determination. And, of course, the hero always wins and everyone lives happily ever after in the end. A bedtime story should always be a happy story, the first familiar step to a night of sweet dreams.

The Glass Mountain

A young princess once lived in a castle made of gold and silver. Though she was as rich as she was beautiful, she was not happy, for a giant eagle had imprisoned her inside the lonely castle. The castle stood atop a steep mountain of pure, smooth glass—a mountain so high that its top touched the clouds. Next to the castle grew a magic tree that bore golden apples. These were very special apples, for only someone who possessed one of them could enter the castle. But the eagle carefully guarded the magic tree and its wonderful fruit, and stopped many knights from reaching the top of the mountain, plucking one of the apples, and entering the castle to rescue the princess.

For seven years, the princess remained locked in her castle, gazing out the window and hoping someone would rescue her. During this time, hundreds of brave knights tried to scale the glass mountain's slippery side. They traveled to the castle from all around the world. Some were lured by the princess's great beauty, while some came looking for fantastic treasure. Others were excited by the challenge of reaching the mountain's steep peak. But none of the knights ever reached the princess.

One knight came very close to reaching the top of the mountain. He fitted the bottoms of his horse's shoes with nails, so the sharp points would dig into the slippery slope. Sparks flew from the horse's hooves as the nails bit into the glass mountainside. But, just as the knight was nearing the top, the great eagle swooped down and scared the horse. Both the horse and the rider slid all the way to the bottom, like so many adventurers before them.

For a long time, no one else tried to climb the mountain. Then, one day, a young man thought he would attempt to rescue the princess. He wasn't a knight or a prince, but an ordinary country boy who didn't even own a horse. He would have to climb the mountain on his own hands and feet.

In order to have a good grip on the slippery slope, he made a pair of gloves that had sharp nails in the fingertips. The gloves made his hands look like steel claws. He pounded more nails through the soles of his boots so they would grip the slick sides of the mountain.

Early one morning the boy began his slow climb up the mountain. Hand over hand he climbed. Slowly and carefully he made progress. A few times he almost lost his grip but saved himself at the last second.

By late afternoon he had almost reached the halfway point up the mountain. His stomach was grumbling with hunger and his mouth was dry with thirst. His arms and legs were losing strength, but he kept moving up the mountain just the same.

Soon the moon rose from behind the mountain, casting its beautiful silver light on the smooth slope. The young man could climb no further and would have to sleep. He dug his hands and feet firmly into the mountainside and fell into a deep slumber.

Around midnight, the giant eagle began circling the mountain, looking for intruders. It saw the young man clinging to the glassy slope and let out a loud "Caw!" trying to frighten the boy. The sound awakened him, but he didn't move a muscle. He lay very, very still, waiting to see what the eagle would do next.

The eagle thought the young man was dead. As it swooped down to knock him off the mountain, the young man grabbed its legs. He hung on for dear life, carefully avoiding the eagle's sharp talons.

The eagle tried to shake him from its legs, but the boy wouldn't let go. The bird flew higher and higher. The boy looked down and gasped—he was miles in the sky!

Unable to lose the young man, the eagle flew to its nest at the top of the glass mountain. Just as the eagle swooped down to its perch, the boy let go and fell safely to the ground near the golden apple tree. Wasting no time, he plucked one of the magic apples. The eagle flew toward him at lightning speed, but the young man hurled the apple at the angry bird, and it vanished in a flash.

From the castle's tower, the princess saw the whole scene. She called down to thank the young man for coming to rescue her. When he saw her in the pale moonlight, he

fell instantly in love with the beautiful princess. He ran around the golden castle looking for an entrance, but it had no door and its only windows were in the tall tower. "How will I ever get in?" he wondered anxiously. Then he remembered the apple's magic powers. He plucked another golden apple from the tree and threw it at the castle wall. Instantly a door appeared. The young man went inside and was amazed. He had never seen a more spectacular castle. The floor of the castle was paved in rare jewels. Sparkling diamonds hung from the ceiling.

But the boy didn't waste time enjoying the riches. The only treasure he wanted was high up in the castle's tower. He ran towards where he had seen the princess in the moonlight. When he reached her, they embraced, and she thanked him for his bravery.

The young man and the princess became man and wife. They spent the rest of their lives high atop the glass mountain, happy as could be.

The Princess
& the Pea

Once upon a time, there lived a handsome prince who was very sad because he could not find a princess to be his bride.

"The princess that I marry must be a true princess," he told his mother, the queen. "She must have good manners and a sense of humor. I'll settle for nothing less."

He traveled around the world seeking a wife. He met many princesses but didn't like any of them. One princess seemed perfect, until he dined with her. Then he discovered that she ate with her fingers and talked with her mouth full of food. Another princess was cruel to her servants. A third princess never laughed or smiled. None of the princesses would make a suitable bride for the young prince. Thinking he'd never find a woman to marry, he returned to his castle, sadder and lonelier than ever.

One night shortly after the prince's return, a fierce storm swept through the kingdom. Rain lashed the castle walls; wind gusted all about. Lightning flashed, and thunder boomed—it was a night to stay indoors.

The king, queen, and prince, safe and warm inside the castle, were eating their dinner when suddenly they heard a loud pounding on the door.

"Who could that be on a miserable night like this one?" asked the king.

A servant ran to see who it was. He slid back the latch and pulled open the heavy wooden door. Standing there was a young woman, soaked to the skin. On either side of her were two servants. They held a piece of cloth over her head trying to keep her dry, but it did no good. The woman's fancy hat was limp and dripping; its feathers and ribbons were a total mess. Her long hair hung like old spaghetti down her back and shoulders. Water ran down her face, dripping off her nose and onto her squishy shoes. Her velvet cloak was ruined and looked like a wet dog.

"Good evening," she said a little sheepishly, a puddle forming around her ankles. "Sorry to trouble you. My carriage broke down outside your castle. May I stay here until it can be repaired?...And may I trouble you for a glass of water?" She started to smile.

For a moment, nobody said anything. Then the prince burst out laughing at the stranger's little joke. The stranger began to laugh, too, and soon everyone was laughing. Everyone, that is, except the queen, who thought the strange woman was terribly common.

The king invited the wet stranger inside and sent his servants to prepare a room for her and her assistants.

"What is your name, young lady?" asked the king.

"I am Fran," she answered. "My father is King Helmut of Gracine."

"Then you're a princess?" asked the prince, who already liked the woman.

"A damp one," she said, "but a true one."

"I doubt that very much," whispered the queen to her husband. "The girl's a mess and a phony."

The castle's servants returned and led the princess to her room. She changed into some dry clothes they had set aside for her and then joined the family for dinner. She proved to be quite charming and well-mannered. The prince quickly grew fond of her, but the queen didn't trust her one bit.

After dinner, the king and queen went to bed, but Fran and the prince stayed up and talked into the wee hours of the night. And, while they talked and laughed, the prince realized that he had found his perfect bride.

The next morning, the king and queen met for breakfast. The prince joined them, too excited by his discovery to sleep any longer. Princess Fran had not yet awakened.

"Mother, Father," said the prince. "I'd like your permission to marry Princess Fran."

"I absolutely forbid it!" said the queen. "She isn't a true princess. Just look at her. Anyone can tell she's just a peasant girl. No princess goes traveling during a storm. And why was she in the neighborhood in the first place? She's just trying to steal our fortune."

"That's not true, Mother," said the prince. "She is every bit a princess. I should know, I've met enough of them these past few months. Besides, I love her!"

The queen and the prince argued back and forth for awhile. Then the king proposed a plan. "Listen," he said. "If she is a true princess, there must be some way of proving it. And if we prove she is true royalty, then there's no reason the marriage can't take place, right?"

"I suppose so," said the queen.

"I suppose so," agreed the prince. "But how do we prove it?"

"I have an idea," replied the queen. "A princess is a delicate creature, sensitive to the

smallest discomfort. Just leave it up to me. I know a sure way of proving that Fran is not a princess."

A short time later, Fran woke up and ate breakfast. When she finished, the prince took her on a tour of the kingdom. Meanwhile, the queen went to work devising a way to test Fran's royal identity. She had her servants replace Fran's bed with twenty brand-new fluffy mattresses stuffed with the softest goose down. They made quite a colossal stack. Under the bottom mattress, the queen placed a single, tiny pea.

"If she is a true princess," thought the queen, "this little pea will make her terribly uncomfortable as she tries to sleep. If she's a fake, she won't even notice it."

Later that evening, the queen explained to Fran that the old bed she had slept on the previous night wasn't befitting a true princess, so she replaced it with a more suitable bed. Imagine Fran's surprise when she saw that her bed now had twenty mattresses on it! She needed a ladder just to climb to the top!

The next morning, the queen sat at the breakfast table with the king and the prince. She told them of how she placed the pea under the princess's mattress. Now was the moment of truth. She couldn't wait to find out how Fran had slept.

Soon, Fran came to the table. She looked terrible, all baggy-eyed and cranky-faced. "What's the matter, child?" asked the king.

"I didn't sleep well," said Fran. "I tossed and turned all night. There must have been something wrong with the new bed. I couldn't get comfortable, no matter how hard I tried."

The queen's face turned bright red when she realized that Fran was truly a princess. The prince began to smile from ear to ear. He jumped out of his seat, ran over, and hugged Fran. Right then and there he asked her to marry him. She said yes, and the couple lived happily together as husband and wife.

The Three Sillies

Once upon a time there lived a farmer, his wife, and their daughter. A young man from town had been paying visits to the daughter for quite some time. The girl's mother and father were fond of the boy and they were sure he was going to ask for her hand in marriage.

One night, when the daughter was old enough to marry, the young man came to the farmhouse to see her. The farmer and his wife were thrilled. "This could be the night he asks to marry our daughter," whispered the farmer's wife.

"Let's hope so," replied the farmer.

The girl's parents wanted to spend some time alone with the young man, just in case he wanted to discuss the couple's marriage with them. So, they sent their daughter down to the cellar to fetch some cider for the visitor. The girl, also thinking this was the greatly anticipated night of her engagement, gladly did as she was told.

In the cellar, she put her pitcher to the spout of a huge cider barrel. As she filled the pitcher, a thought struck her: "If I marry this man and we have children, what will we name them?"

This question distressed the girl. She began reciting boys' names—"Percival...Virgil... Othniel..."—but she didn't like any of them. So she tried some girls' names—"Desdemona...Winnifred... Gertrude..." No, none of them seemed right either.

Lost in her thoughts, she forgot to turn off the spout on the cider barrel. The cider poured out of the barrel, overflowed her pitcher, and spilled onto the floor. But she didn't even notice the mess. She just racked her brain trying to think of names for her children.

Soon her mother came down to the cellar, wondering what was taking her daughter so long.

"Mother," said the daughter, "I was just thinking. If I marry that young man upstairs, and we have children, what we will name them?"

"Hmm..." replied her mother, "let me think about that with you." And she sat down on the stairs, while the cider kept pouring onto the floor.

After a while the farmer came downstairs to see what was keeping his wife and daughter. He found them sitting in the cellar, lost in thought.

"What's the matter?" he asked.

"Father," said the daughter, "Mother and I were just thinking. If I marry that young man upstairs, and we have children, what will we name them?"

"That's an important question," said the farmer. "Let me help you answer it." So he joined them on the cellar steps. By now, the

cellar was almost ankle deep with sweet cider, but the threesome barely noticed.

After a while, the young visitor, left alone upstairs at the table for so long, grew curious about what had become of his hosts. He went to the cellar and found them sitting knee-deep in cider, gazing into space.

"What is the matter?" he asked, reaching over and closing the spout on the near-empty cider barrel.

"If my daughter marries you," said the father, "and you have children, what will you name them?"

"You people are the silliest folks I've ever met," said the young man. "I haven't even said I wished to marry your daughter. But I'll tell you what. I have to do some traveling for a few weeks. While I'm away, if I can find three people sillier than you, I'll happily marry your daughter." Saying that, the young man left.

Early the next day, he began his travels. He hadn't gone far before he came upon a woman who was trying to push a pig up the trunk of an oak tree.

"What are you doing?" the young man asked. He'd never seen such a thing in his life.

"This here's my prize pig," said the woman. "I want to feed her acorns to make her nice and fat, but I can't get her to climb the tree and get to them."

The young man tried not to laugh out loud. "With all due respect, ma'am," he said, "I think you'll have better luck climbing the tree yourself and shaking the acorns to the

ground. Then your pig will find them."

"Oh!" exclaimed the woman. "I hadn't thought of that. Thank you, wise stranger."

"That's one silly," thought the young man to himself as he continued down the road.

By nightfall he arrived in a small town. In the center of town, he saw an old man crawling around on his hands and knees under a street lamp, as if he were looking for something. "Have you lost something?" asked the young man. "Perhaps I can help you find it."

"Yes," said the old man, looking up. "I lost a gold coin." He continued searching every inch of ground under the street light.

"Are you certain you dropped it here?" asked the young man.

"I didn't drop it here," said the old man, this time without looking up. "I dropped it in the woods. It's just that the light is much better here, so it'll be easier to find."

The young man was so astonished he didn't know what to say. He just kept going on his way, thinking, "That's silly number two."

The young man was very tired so after supper he got a room in the town's inn. He slept well, but was awakened very early the next morning by the sounds of pounding and crashing coming from the next room. He put on some clothes and knocked on his neighbor's door.

The door opened, and, much to the young man's surprise, another man stood on the other side of the threshold in his underwear.

"Come in," said the other man. "You must be an early riser since you're already wearing your pants. It takes me hours to put mine on right. Excuse me

a moment while I try again."

The man's trousers were hanging on the closet doorknob on the other side of the room. He took a running start and tried to leap into them. But he failed to get even one leg into his pants and came crashing to the floor. The young man watched him try this again and again. Each time the man was sure that he'd be able to jump into his trousers, and each time he landed in a heap on the floor with his pants still hanging in the closet.

"Excuse me," said the young man. "You may find the trousers easier to put on if you hold them in your hands and step into them one leg at a time."

"Well, I never thought of that!" said the man in his underwear. "Thanks for your help."

The young man left the room. "That's silly number three!" he said to himself, smiling at all the silliness he had encountered on his journey. After breakfast, he returned to the farmer's house, asked for the daughter's hand in marriage, and the two lived happily ever after.

The Enchanted Watch

There once lived a wealthy man and his three sons. The oldest son was wise and adventurous and wanted to travel. When he grew old enough to venture out on his own, his father gave him a ship, and the young man sailed off to explore the world. A little more than a year later, he returned home from his travels a happy—and very wealthy—young man.

The father was proud of his son's success, so he threw a large party in his honor. He hired clowns, acrobats, and magicians to perform for his son's entertainment. He served his son's favorite foods and invited all of his son's friends to welcome him home.

The second son, happy for his older brother's success, asked his father for permission to travel across the sea. This son was just as wise and sensible as his older brother, so his father gave him a ship to sail and sent him on his way.

A year later, the second son returned, just as successful as the first. To honor him, the father threw another party, as grand as the first.

Now it was the third son's turn to travel. His name was Johnny, and he wasn't as sensible as his two brothers. In fact, his father thought him to be a bit of a fool. But now he was old enough to see the world on his own, so he asked his father for a ship. Like his brothers, he hoped to find his fortune in an exotic land.

Johnny's father didn't think his traveling was such a good idea. He believed Johnny would get himself into danger or trouble, but he also had a small hope that seeing the world would teach Johnny some sense. So he gave Johnny a small boat, wondering whether he'd ever see his son again.

Johnny sailed off and soon arrived in a strange land. He saw a group of farmers chasing after a dog that had been attacking their sheep. "Please," said Johnny, "let me take the dog with me, and it will never bother you again."

The farmers gave him the dog, and Johnny went on his way. A bit later, he saw a woman with a rolling pin chasing a cat who had been stealing her chickens. "Please," said Johnny, "let me take the cat with me on my ship, and it will never bother you again."

The woman stopped chasing the cat. Johnny called to it, and it jumped into his arms, thankful for the rescue.

As Johnny, the dog, and the cat traveled, they happened upon a man about to kill a snake for stealing eggs. "Please," said Johnny, "let me take the snake with me, and it will never bother you again."

The man gave the snake to Johnny and the foursome went on their way.

Suddenly, the snake said, "Thank you for saving my life. If you follow me, I'll take you to meet my king. He'll reward you for your kindness with a magic watch. Just rub the watch and it will give you whatever you wish."

Johnny, the dog, and the cat followed the snake into a huge hole in the ground. There they met the king of the snakes, who cheerfully gave Johnny the magic watch. Johnny thanked the king, said good-bye to his new snake friend, and then climbed back outside with the dog and the cat.

Once outside, Johnny tested the magic watch. "Let's have a nice, big lunch," he said to the dog and the cat. He rubbed the watch and instantly they had all the meat and bread and cider and milk they could possibly ever want. Johnny was overjoyed that the watch truly had magical powers.

When evening came the three travelers wanted to rest, so Johnny rubbed the watch again and found himself and his companions in a cozy inn with a comfortable bed. The next morning when he awoke, he said to the dog and the cat, "With this watch, I'm just as successful as my brothers. So, let's go to my father's house and make him proud of me."

Johnny, the dog, and the cat sailed to Johnny's home. His father wasn't pleased, for all Johnny had to show for his travels were a dog, a cat, and a watch. His father yelled at him for being a fool and wouldn't throw a party to celebrate his return.

A few days later, Johnny became bored with hanging around the same old house. "Wouldn't it be nice if the house was bigger?" he thought.

He took the enchanted watch out of his pocket, made his wish, and with a lurch the house began to grow. Then Johnny wished for nicer furniture, and it appeared in a flash. His father, who was just returning home from an errand, was astonished. He ran to Johnny to find out what had happened. Johnny didn't tell him about the watch, but simply said, "You didn't host a party for me when I returned from my trip, so I'm having one for myself. Let's invite the king, the queen, and the princess. Outside you'll find a coach made of solid gold in which they may ride royally."

Upon looking out the side of his house, his father was amazed to see a golden coach, just as Johnny had said. The father drove the coach to the castle to call on the royal family. The king and queen had never seen such a beautiful coach, and they gladly accepted the invitation. The royal family climbed into the coach, and Johnny's father drove them to his house. Meanwhile, Johnny used the magic watch to turn all the cobblestone streets to polished white marble so their ride would be as smooth as could be.

When they arrived at the house, they found a delicious banquet awaiting them in a huge hall. The royal family had never tasted better food. By dessert, the king asked Johnny's father if he would agree to the marriage of Johnny and his daughter, the princess. Naturally, Johnny's father said yes and the two families began planning the wedding.

After their marriage, Johnny's watch provided his new bride with everything she could possibly want. But she had a ferocious, greedy appetite for fine things. No matter how much she had, she always wanted more—more clothes, a bigger house, rare gems. Johnny spent all of his time trying to make his young bride happy, but she wouldn't be content until she could make the magic work for herself.

One day, when Johnny was away from home, the princess stole the watch. With it she wished that a beautiful island with a magnificent palace might rise from the sea. Then she wished for a long bridge so she could cross the sea to the island. She rubbed the watch and her wishes appeared before her eyes. She crossed the bridge to the island, rubbed the watch again, and the bridge vanished.

When Johnny realized his wife had run away with his watch, he immediately began searching for her. When he heard of a strange new island with a magnificent new castle on it, he knew that his wife must be there.

He said to his dog, "You're a strong swimmer. I'd like you to swim to that island to find my wife and my watch."

Then he said to his cat, "You, little one, must ride on his back. I need you to sneak into the castle and retrieve my watch."

The dog and the cat crossed the sea, arrived at the castle, and sneaked inside. But the princess saw them from her castle window. She locked the watch in the cellar to keep it safe from the intruders. But the crafty cat was able to sneak into the locked room. She held the watch in her mouth and waited patiently until the princess—thinking the dog and cat had left the island—came back to retrieve it. As soon as

the princess opened the door, the cat bolted for the opening with the watch clutched between her teeth. She jumped on the dog's back. "Let's get out of here!" she cried, and the dog dove into the sea.

The dog and cat returned the watch to Johnny. Though it was wet from the journey, its magic still worked just fine. Johnny wished that the princess would be returned safely to her parents and for her to forget all about the magic watch. Then he wished all the magnificent things he'd ever wished for were gone. Once he returned to his simple life, he lived happily ever after.

King Midas

Once there lived a powerful king who ruled over a vast empire. His name was Midas. He was a fair ruler, and his people liked him. While he ruled there was great happiness and wealth in the land.

But King Midas had one problem: his weakness for gold. Even though he was one of the richest kings in the world, he always wanted more gold. He simply couldn't get enough of the shimmering metal. He would trade grain for it. He would trade cattle for it. He would send prospectors to the ends of the earth to find new gold mines. The castle's vaults brimmed with the stuff. His buttons and doorknobs and teaspoons and goblets all were made of gold. He had so much gold that he was running out of places to keep it. Yet nothing satisfied his hunger. "More gold!" he cried. "I must have more gold!"

One day Midas went to visit a fortuneteller. She was an old, kindly woman with a scratchy voice and soft hands. "I know why you have come to visit me, King Midas," she said. "You wish to find a way to get more gold."

"It doesn't take a fortuneteller to guess that," smiled Midas. "Everyone knows how much I adore gold."

"Ahh!" said the old woman. "But I know things others don't. For example, I know that you're entitled to one wish. Every king gets one, you know, as long as he rules wisely. And, even though you're a little crazy about gold, no one can deny that you're a good king deserving of your wish."

"So you mean I can wish for anything I want?" asked Midas, very excited by the idea.

"Anything at all," said the fortuneteller. "But be careful what you wish for. Sometimes the thing you want the most is what causes you the most harm."

King Midas, of course, heard none of this warning. His head was spinning with visions of solid gold mountains so high that their peaks were capped with snow. His imagination conjured forests of shimmering trees that shed gold leaves in autumn. He dreamed about strolling down golden streets in his golden shoes. The possibilities were endless. He was so excited that he almost couldn't speak.

"I know what I want my wish to be!" he suddenly blurted.

"Be absolutely certain now," warned the fortuneteller. "With big wishes come big complications."

"Oh, of course," said the king, not listening to the woman's warning. "Here's my wish: I wish that everything I touch would turn to solid gold." Midas beamed with pleasure at the thought of it.

"Hmm," said the fortuneteller, frowning.

"If that's your wish, there's nothing more to say, except good luck. I grant you this wish."

Midas picked up a log from the hearth just to test his new powers. Sure enough, as soon as he touched it, it turned to solid gold. "Wow!" he exclaimed. "That's amazing!" He turned to the old fortuneteller. "You may keep that as payment for your services," he told her. "And thank you for your help." He reached out to shake the old woman's hand, but she turned away before he could touch her. "Oops! Sorry," he said, sheepishly. "Close call. I almost turned you to gold."

Midas left the fortuneteller's house, and as he did so, he turned the doorknob and even the door to gold. "Well, I'm better off for the king's visit," thought the old woman. "But I'm not so sure the king is."

King Midas rode his now-golden chariot down the now-golden street to his castle. He was as happy as he could be. Along the way he would stop and turn trees and pebbles into gold. He spied a turtle crossing the road, so he turned it into gold as well and was delighted with the result. "What a splendid gift for my daughter!" he thought to himself. If there was one thing Midas loved more than gold, it was his daughter.

As the king rode to his castle, the townspeople began to notice that the street had turned to gold. They greedily started chopping it apart with axes and picks in order to have some for themselves.

Before long, the road was pitted and torn apart and full of potholes. "Hmm," thought the king, "I'll have to pass a law about that." He reached for his pen and writing tablet to make a note to himself, but they both turned into gold as soon as he laid a finger on them.

Soon he arrived at the castle, which, of course, he turned into gold. By now it was lunch time and the king was hungry. The royal chef prepared the king's dining table with loaves of fresh bread, wheels of fine cheeses, slabs of delicious meat, and ripe, juicy fruit. The king pulled his suddenly golden chair up to the suddenly golden table and reached for the bread. It immediately turned to gold. The king laughed at the spectacle. He tried using his other hand to grab an apple. It, too, turned to gold. Soon he had turned all the meat, cheeses, and even his water into gold.

Midas was no longer amused. "I'm going to starve to death!" he cried. He tried covering his hands with gloves, but it didn't help. Finally, he ordered one of his servants to cut up his food and feed him as if he were a little child.

"It's worth the trouble," he thought to himself, "if it means I can turn whatever I want into gold."

He had just finished eating, when he heard his daughter return from her trip into town. King Midas couldn't wait to see her and give her the golden turtle. As he went to get the gift, his daughter came rushing in to greet him. Before he could stop her, she gave him a hug and turned instantly into a golden statue.

"Look what I've done to my precious daughter!" cried the king as he pried himself loose from her golden grip. "This gift has become a curse. I must be rid of it!"

He called for his carriage and rode back to the fortuneteller. The trip was difficult because the roads were all torn up from the townspeople's digging. Upon his arrival, he burst through the golden door and pleaded with the fortuneteller, "You must free me of this golden touch. It's destroying my life!"

"I told you so," scolded the old woman. "But I think I can help you. Go down to the river, take off all your clothes, and dive into the water. Your golden gift will be washed away."

King Midas thanked the fortuneteller and ran to the river. He did as she instructed. When he jumped into the water, it shimmered all around him like liquid gold, and then the current washed the sparkling water down-stream.

When he left the river, the sandy banks were flecked with gold. Midas ran to the nearest tree and touched its bark, but it remained a tree. He picked up a rock, but it stayed a rock. He began to dance and sing happily rid of his gift. But then he remembered his daughter and grew sad. He traveled back home with great heaviness in his heart. But, a surprise awaited him when he entered the castle door.

"Father!" cried his daughter.

"Thank heavens!" said the king. "You've changed back."

He spread his arms out wide as his daughter came running toward him. She stopped in her tracks just before wrapping her arms around his middle.

"It's okay," he assured her, "the curse is gone now." Then he hugged her with all his might. He realized that he already had a gift much greater than all the gold in the world.

Stone Soup

A fierce war had just ended, and a soldier weary from battle was making the long journey home to his family. His travels led him to many different places as he walked up hills and down dales, through great cities and small towns. He'd seen many things, but more than anything, he wanted to see his family.

Before long he ran out of money and his stomach began to feel as empty as his pockets. While traveling on the road, he would ask people he met if they could spare some food, but nobody would share with him.

One day he came to a village. It was near dinnertime, and the smell of home-cooking filled the air, reminding him of the meals he had shared with his own family so long ago. The soldier knocked on the door of a pleasant-looking cottage. A plump woman answered the door.

"Please ma'am," said the hungry soldier, "could you spare a morsel for a weary soldier?"

"The war has been hard on us, too," said the woman. "Food is scarce. We can't spare a bite." And she abruptly closed her door.

He went to the next house. A robust man answered his knock.

"Sorry, young lad," he said. "The crops have been poor this year. Our cupboard is empty."

"The people in this village are not very generous," said the soldier to himself after visiting several more houses, without anyone offering him a bite to eat. "Perhaps I'll have better luck down the road."

He went from village to village, door to door, asking people for some food. But nobody could spare anything—not an apple, not a turnip green, not even a moldy slice of bread or a single dried bean.

As he left town he also left his hope for any help behind him. "What's to become of me?" he asked himself as he wandered down the road, kicking a stone. "I must think of a way to get food, or I will surely starve." He pondered what to do but his stomach rumbled so loudly that he could barely think. "If only I could eat stones," he thought, "then I could feast like a king." The thought made him smile as he continued kicking a round stone down the road with his heavy boot.

An idea slowly formed in the soldier's head as he approached the next village. He wiped off the stone, wrapped it neatly in his handkerchief, and put it in his pocket.

After arriving in the village, the soldier knocked on the door of the house closest to the center of town. "Have you the space for a weary soldier to rest his bones?" he asked the old woman who answered the door. "You may rest here on the stoop if you wish," said the woman, "but don't hope for any more than that. There's nobody home but me, and I can't let you in."

"Fair enough," said the soldier.

"And if you're expecting me to feed you, you're sorely mistaken," continued the woman. "I've not a crumb to spare. I dare say the same holds true for everyone in this village. The season has been hard and food is scarce. So I suggest you rest your feet here for a few moments, if you must, then move on."

"No food, you say?" replied the soldier. "That is a sad thing for you and this village. But it's a good thing I arrived here when I did, for I myself am in no need of food. I carry with me a magical stone which can turn a pot of hot water into the most delicious soup."

"Come on," laughed the woman, "no stone can do that. You'll have to show me that fancy trick if you expect me to believe it."

"I'll be more than happy to show you," said the soldier. He pulled the stone from his pocket and carefully unwrapped it. "Fetch me a pot of water, and we'll enjoy the soup together."

The woman wasted no time bringing him her largest cauldron. She built a fire outside while the soldier filled the pot with water from the well. Then he dropped the stone into the water—kerplunk!—and set the pot over the fire.

When the water was near boiling, the woman brought the soldier a ladle so he could sample the brew. "It's a nice broth," said the soldier, "but any soup is better with a little salt and pepper." The woman rushed back to her house and brought out the salt and pepper. The soldier added them both and stirred the bubbling liquid.

Soon other people from the village stopped by wondering what the stranger was doing. "He's making soup from a stone," the woman told them, and they had to stay and watch for they couldn't believe it.

"So far, so good," said the soldier, tasting the soup. "But any soup is better with a few carrots thrown in." As soon as he said this, one of the villagers rushed home and returned with a bunch of carrots.

After a few more minutes of stirring, the soldier sampled the soup again. "Mmm," he said, "the soup is almost ready. But with a few beans, it would be a soup anyone would be proud to serve to guests."

Upon hearing this, someone from the crowd instantly ran home and brought him some beans. The crowd continued to gather, watching the soldier make soup out of a stone. Every few minutes, he would sample the soup and

suggest another ingredient that would make the concoction a little better.

"An onion would make this soup truly special," he said, and a villager brought him an onion. "Some greens would give the soup a nice color," he said, and someone else brought him greens. "A bone with some meat left on it would make this stone soup a feast for even royalty," he said, and one of the villagers suddenly found he could spare a bone for the magic soup.

Little by little, the villagers—who had proclaimed earlier that they had not a morsel of food to spare—added ingredients to the soup. At last the soldier took one final taste, smiled broadly, and declared it a masterpiece. He ladled bowls of the steaming concoction for himself and the woman. As they ate their fill, the villagers lined up to sample spoonfuls out of the pot.

Everyone was just amazed. The soldier had indeed made delicious soup with nothing more than a pot of water and a magical stone.

The Little Red Hen

One day, while Little Red Hen scratched around the dusty barnyard with her little yellow chicks, she found some grains of wheat.

"Cluck, cluck, cluck," said Little Red Hen happily. "I've found some grains of wheat. Now I can plant them."

She knew that planting can be hard work, so she asked her friends to help. First, she went to Little White Duck. "Cluck, cluck, cluck," said Little Red Hen, "will you help me plant my wheat?"

"Quack, quack, quack," said Little White Duck. "I can't help you plant your wheat. I have to swim in my cool, blue lake. I don't have time to help you."

So Little Red Hen went to ask Big Brown Cow for help.

"Moo, moo, moo," said Big Brown Cow. "I can't help you plant your wheat, Little Red Hen. I have a big field of green clover to munch on. I'm much too busy to plant your wheat with you."

Next, she visited Fat Pink Pig to ask for his help.

"Oink, oink, oink," said Fat Pink Pig. "I can't help you today, Little Red Hen. I've got a gooey puddle of mud that needs my attention."

Little Red Hen then paid a visit to Little Gray Dog, but he was busy, too.

"Woof, woof, woof," said Little Gray Dog. "I'd like to help you plant your wheat, but I can't. I've got to spend the day chasing my tail."

Finally, Little Red Hen asked Big Black Cat for her help.

"Mew, mew, mew," said Big Black Cat. "Sorry, I can't help you, Little Red Hen. I have to tend to this sunny porch. But, if you wish, I'll watch your chicks while you go to work."

"Cluck, cluck, cluck," said Little Red Hen, noticing the cat licking her chops. "Thank you, Big Black Cat, but I prefer that my chicks come with me."

With no one to help her plant her wheat, Little Red Hen did the job by herself. She watched it and watered it, and as the weeks went by, the wheat grew big and tall. Soon it was time to cut the golden stalks.

"Cluck, cluck, cluck," said Little Red Hen. "Who will help me cut the wheat?" Again, she asked her friends for help.

"Quack, quack, quack," said Little White Duck. "I'd love to help you, but I can't. I have more swimming to do."

"Moo, moo, moo," said Big Brown Cow. "Not today, Little Red Hen. The clover's in bloom, and I have some serious grazing to do."

"Oink, oink, oink," said Fat Pink Pig. "Thanks for the invitation to cut wheat with you, but there's a new mud puddle that I need to explore. I can't help you, Little Red Hen."

"Woof, woof, woof," said Little Gray Dog. "I'm not able to help. I still haven't caught up with my tail."

"Mew, mew, mew," said Big Black Cat. "Sorry, Little Red Hen, I'm busy today. I've got to wash my hair."

With no one to help her cut her wheat, Little Red Hen did the job by herself. She gathered the wheat together into tall, golden bundles. Now it was time to thresh the wheat, separating the tender kernels from the tough stems.

"Cluck, cluck, cluck," said Little Red Hen, looking for help from her friends. "Who will help me thresh the wheat?"

"Quack, quack, quack," said Little White Duck. "I can't help you. I've got swimming practice."

"Moo, moo, moo," said Big Brown Cow. "I can't help you. I've got important fields to graze."

"Oink, oink, oink," said Fat Pink Pig. "I can't help you, either. I found some new filth in which I really need to play."

"Woof, woof, woof," said Little Gray Dog. "I'd like to help you, but I can't. I've got to chase my shadow."

"Mew, mew, mew," said Big Black Cat. "Sorry I can't help you. I just had my claws done."

So Little Red Hen had to thresh the wheat herself. Luckily, by now her chicks were old enough to help her. It took a long time, but when the job was done, she had a tidy pile of plump wheat kernels. Her chicks wanted to eat some right away, but she told them that there was more work to be done. Now they had to grind the wheat into flour. She thought that maybe this time her friends would help.

"Cluck, cluck, cluck," said Little Red Hen. "Who will help me grind the wheat?"

"Quack, quack, quack," said Little White Duck. "Not I. I've got to work on my backstroke."

"Moo, moo, moo," said Big Brown Cow. "Not I. I've got some serious munching to do."

"Oink, oink, oink," said Fat Pink Pig. "Not I. I've got to take a mud bath."

"Woof, woof, woof," said Little Gray Dog. "I can't help you either. I still haven't caught my shadow."

"Mew, mew, mew," said Big Black Cat. "I'm busy too. It's time for my nap."

So, Little Red Hen and her chicks ground the wheat into flour all by themselves. Now she was ready to make bread with the flour. Would any of her friends help? It couldn't hurt to ask.

"Cluck, cluck, cluck," said Little Red Hen. "Who will help me bake my bread?"

"Quack, quack, quack," said Little White Duck. "I can't help you. Sorry."

"Moo, moo, moo," said Big Brown Cow. "I'm not available. Sorry."

"Oink, oink, oink," said Fat Pink Pig. "Sorry, I'm busy."

"Woof, woof, woof," said Little Gray Dog. "Not this time. Sorry."

"Mew, mew, mew," said Big Black Cat. "Sorry, I have other plans."

So Little Red Hen and her chicks baked the bread themselves. Soon its delicious smell filled the barnyard, making everyone's mouth water. Slowly, all of Little Red Hen's friends began gathering around her warm kitchen. Before long, the bread was done, and Little Red Hen pulled two golden, steamy loaves out of the oven.

"Cluck, cluck, cluck," said Little Red Hen, smiling. "Who will help me eat my bread?"

"Quack, quack, quack," said Little White Duck. "I will!"

"Moo, moo, moo," said Big Brown Cow. "I will!"

"Oink, oink, oink," said Fat Pink Pig. "I will!"

"Woof, woof, woof," said Little Gray Dog. "I will!"

"Mew, mew, mew," said Big Black Cat. "I will!"

"Cluck! Cluck! Cluck! Oh, no you won't!" said Little Red Hen. "Because you didn't help me plant the wheat, cut the stalks, thresh the grain, grind the flour, or bake the bread, you don't deserve to eat any. It's just for me and my chicks. Next time, perhaps you'll be a little more helpful."

Little Red Hen and her chicks ate their fill of the warm bread and saved the rest for later.

The Lion and the Mouse

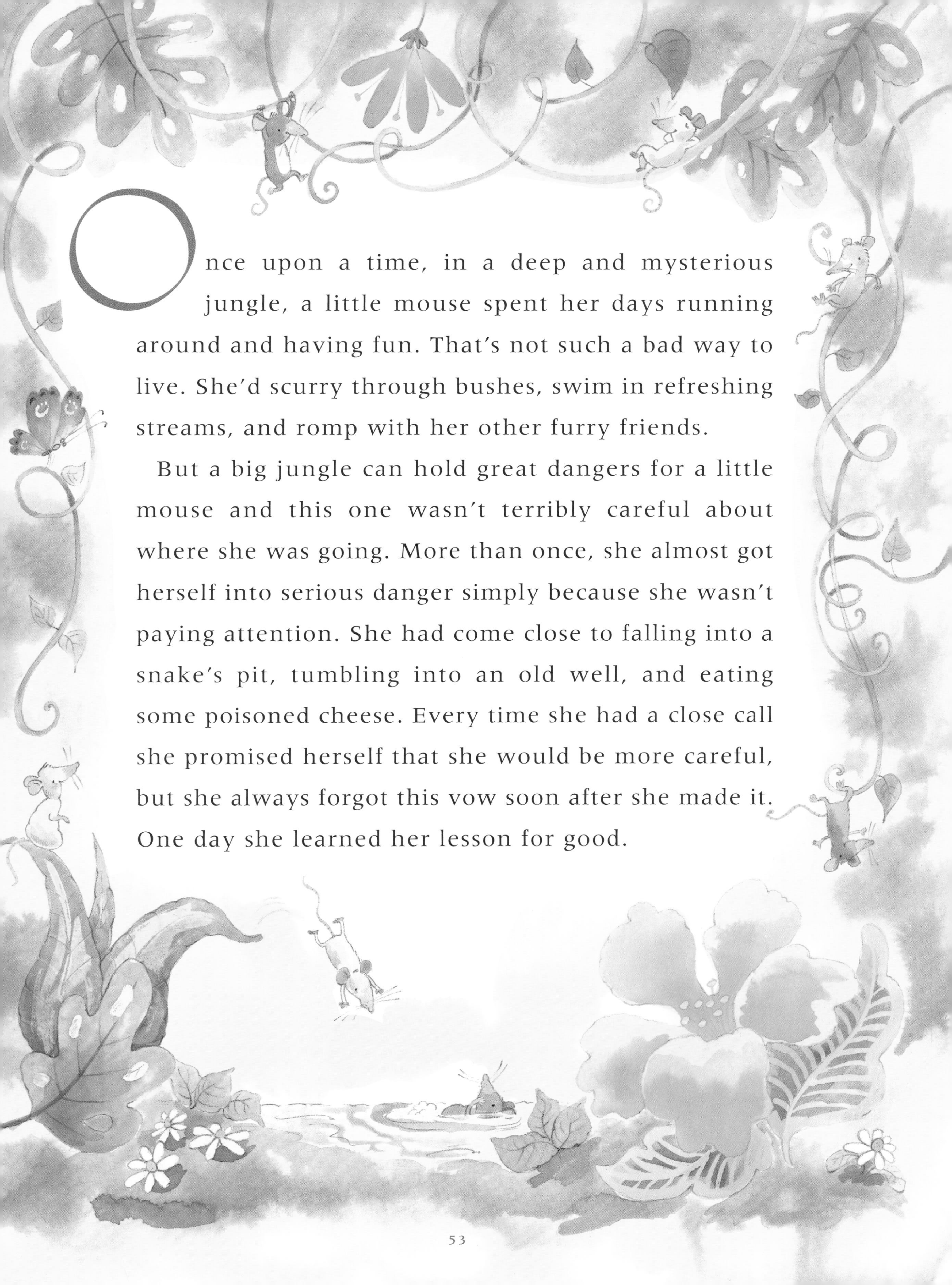

Once upon a time, in a deep and mysterious jungle, a little mouse spent her days running around and having fun. That's not such a bad way to live. She'd scurry through bushes, swim in refreshing streams, and romp with her other furry friends.

But a big jungle can hold great dangers for a little mouse and this one wasn't terribly careful about where she was going. More than once, she almost got herself into serious danger simply because she wasn't paying attention. She had come close to falling into a snake's pit, tumbling into an old well, and eating some poisoned cheese. Every time she had a close call she promised herself that she would be more careful, but she always forgot this vow soon after she made it. One day she learned her lesson for good.

It was a bright, sunny day like any other, and the little mouse was chasing some feathery seeds the wind was blowing about the jungle. As usual, she didn't watch where she was going, and ran right onto a lion's muscular paw as he lay sleeping in the sun.

Lions don't sleep heavily, and this one was no exception. Feeling the little mouse on his paw, the lion swiftly lifted his other paw and trapped the mouse beneath it.

"What bold creature dares disturb my nap?" roared the lion.

The little mouse, shaking with fear, squeezed her head out from beneath the lion's paw and said, "I'm sorry, Mr. Lion. I didn't mean to wake you."

"I was having the nicest dream," said the lion, "and you interrupted it."

"It was an accident," squeaked the mouse. "I'm so terribly sorry. It won't ever happen again."

"I don't care if it was an accident or not," roared the lion. "But you're right—it won't happen again...because I'm going to eat you!"

"Oh! Please don't do that, Mr. Lion," pleaded the mouse, now trembling more than ever. "I'm sure I don't taste very good. And besides, if you let me go, perhaps someday I can repay your kindness."

The mouse's plea made the lion laugh. "How can a tiny creature like you ever help the King of Beasts?" he said. "You're being ridiculous."

"Well," said the mouse, "stranger things have happened."

"Yes, I suppose so," agreed the lion. "And I admire your spirit, little one. Okay. I'll let you go, but just this once. If you ever awaken me again, that'll be the last of you." With that, he lifted his paw, freeing the mouse.

"Oh thank you, Mr. Lion," said the mouse, scurrying off. "You won't be sorry!"

From then on, the mouse played more carefully and she made sure to keep quiet and to stay away from the lion during his nap time. One day, many weeks after their first encounter, while she was out searching for seeds to eat, the mouse heard a sad and terrible roar.

"That sounds like my friend, the lion," she said. "He may need my help."

She scurried through the thick, green jungle, following the awful sounds of the lion's cry.

Soon the mouse saw him and she couldn't believe her eyes—there was the King of Beasts, caught in a hunter's trap! He was unable to escape from the heavy net of ropes that had fallen over him.

The mouse ran over to him. "Don't worry," she said to the struggling lion. "Now's my chance to repay the debt I owe you."

"How can you help me, little one?" moaned the lion. "My time is up! Soon the hunter will return, and I'll be done for sure!"

"Don't even think that," replied the mouse. "Just keep still and watch me work. You'll be free in no time."

The little mouse set to work gnawing through the ropes. Before long, she made a hole in the net large enough for the lion's escape. He quickly crawled out the opening and stretched his long body. Free once again, the lion thanked the mouse for keeping her promise and saving his life. He also apologized for doubting that such a little mouse could think up such a clever scheme.

"It only goes to show you," said the lion, "you never know when little friends can help you escape from big trouble."